Rock Star Lawyer
An Oliver Boys Rockstar Romance
by
Rose Bak

Rock Star Lawyer

Oliver Boys Band, Volume 5

Rose Bak

Published by Rose Bak, 2022.

Table of Contents

ROCK STAR LAWYER

© 2022 by Rose Bak

Cover Design by Paper or Pixels[1]

---

1.   https://paperorpixels.com/

About this Book

They come from two different worlds, but they'll work together to help raise money for Ukraine.

Once upon a time, Jayden Oliver was rock music royalty. The Oliver Boys was the most popular boy band in a generation until they stepped away to return to a normal life. Now Jayden is a lawyer, quietly using his law degree to help people. When his boss asks him to help plan a benefit concert to support Ukrainian refugees, he jumps at the chance to get involved.

Alona Pavlenko grew up steeped in the culture of her people. The daughter of Ukrainian refugees has no time or interest in the fancy billionaire lifestyle of the man she's planning a concert with. She's determined to resist his flirting. But to her shock, she realizes that Jayden is just as down to earth and as committed to family as she is.

But when the tabloids report that Jayden and his brothers are returning to their rock & roll lifestyle, Alona doesn't want any part of it. Can he convince her that the only thing that's important to him is a life with Alona?

"Rock Star Lawyer" is book five of the "Oliver Boys Rockstar Romance" series. This steamy standalone features a strong and independent woman, a man who believes in love at first sight, and lots of nosy family members determined to matchmake them into their happily ever after.

Dedication

To the brave people of Ukraine, you are my heroes. Slava Ukraini!

Join My Mailing List

Join Rose Bak's mailing list at https://bit.ly/rosebaknewsletter. You'll get a free book and be the first to hear about all the latest releases and special sales.

Jayden

"Do you have a minute?"

Jayden looked up as his boss, Dave Macetti, entered his office. The men worked together at the Davis, Lang & White law firm, where Jayden was a second year associate. Dave sat down with a groan.

"You OK?"

"Yeah thanks, I'm just sore. My wife convinced me to train for a marathon with her, and we ran twenty miles yesterday."

He lowered his voice, as if he was afraid that someone would hear him. "I don't like running that far. I wanted to die."

Jayden laughed. "Then why are you doing it?"

"Because Jenny asked me to," he said, as if that explained everything. And perhaps it did.

"But I didn't come in here to whine about my sore calves. I wanted to talk to you about a new charity project the firm is taking on."

Jayden pulled out a fresh legal pad and a pen so he could take notes. The firm where they worked was very committed to giving back to the community and there was always a pro bono case or a fundraising effort underway for the team to get involved with. It was one of the things that attracted him to the firm when he got out of law school.

"We're partnering with RUC to put on a benefit concert for humanitarian relief for Ukrainians."

"RUC?" Jayden asked.

"Resettled Ukrainians of Chicago, it's a refugee resettlement organization that's been helping Ukrainians settle in the Chicagoland area for over fifty years."

"Wow. OK, so what do you need? A donation?"

"I was hoping you would be willing to co-chair the benefit concert planning committee."

"Me? Why?"

A slight flush rose up Dave's face. "We were hoping to get some big names at the concert to raise a lot of money, even though it's short notice," Dave explained. "I know you don't like to talk about this at work, but given your performance background, we thought you'd have the connections we need to pull this off and make it a success. None of the rest of us know anything about planning a concert, especially one as big as we hope this one will be."

It was an open secret that the law was Jayden's second career. When he was younger, he and his three older brothers had created a band that played at parties and venues around their small hometown in Kansas. When Jayden was nineteen, an L.A. music producer had discovered the group while they were performing at a local bar and offered them a recording contract on the spot. What followed was a whirlwind rise to fame. The Oliver Boys became one of the biggest "boy bands" of their generation, filling up stadiums around the world.

But fame wasn't all it was cracked up to be. Somewhere along the line, Jayden and his brothers got tired of the wild parties, alcohol, and groupies. When the grandparents who raised them died within six months of each other, the brothers decided to retire. Fame had lost its luster, and they all had more money than they could ever spend. After one last "farewell" tour they ended their successful music careers and returned to regular life.

Jim and Justin returned to Kansas, Jim to teach high school and Justin to write songs for other artists. Their oldest brother Johnny wrote a thriller and fell in love with his editor, moving to New York City to live with her while he wrote full-time. And Jayden moved to Chicago for college and law school before getting a job here at the law firm.

"Sure, I can co-chair," Jayden readily agreed. "I can also see if I can drag my brothers to Chicago to play a set. We've been talking about doing a reunion show anyway."

"That would be great," Dave said approvingly. "No pressure though. The partners would like you to represent us as co-chair either way."

"Understood."

"You'll be working with the events coordinator for RUC, a woman named Alona Pavlenko." Dave slid a piece of paper across his desk. "Here's her contact information as well as what the firm agreed to do in terms of scope of work. Your first planning meeting is...," he looked at his watch, "in about thirty minutes."

"Thirty minutes?" Jayden sputtered.

Dave nodded. "Yeah, sorry for the short notice. We thought Miles had talked to you about it last week before he left on vacation, but I realized this morning that he must have forgotten. We made arrangements for you to meet Ms. Pavlenko here in your office. Your assistant already put it in your schedule."

Jayden nodded. "Sounds good."

"Thanks for doing this, man. I appreciate you supporting the cause."

"Glad to help. What's happening over there is terrible, and honestly I've been looking for a way to help. My grandma was Ukrainian."

Dave slowly stood up, suppressing a groan. "That's awesome Jayden. The firm's resources are at your disposal. Feel free to pull in whoever you need to make this work."

"You got it. Thanks, Dave."

Alona

Alona smoothed her knee-length skirt down and looked around the lobby. Like every law office she'd ever been in, the furnishings were expensive and understated, making her feel like a poor interloper. It was a far cry from the threadbare offices of the charity she worked at.

She glanced at the tiny blonde Barbie-doll wannabe at the desk and tried not to feel insecure. Over the years she'd come to terms with the fact that she'd never be skinny and perfect like the receptionist. Her mother had always told her that she came from "peasant stock" which was code for having genes that kept a death grip on every calorie she consumed to fight off famine.

There wasn't a lot of famine here in Chicago, but tell that to her thighs. No amount of dieting had ever shrunk her natural curves, and somewhere in her late twenties she'd resolved to just accept them. She was fit and knew how to dress to accentuate her figure. She'd learned to love herself despite her curvy body, and with that came a self-confidence that drew people to her. She knew she wasn't everyone's cup of tea, but she'd had her fair share of boyfriends.

"Miss, um, Pav, um, len-ko?"

She tried not to grimace at the mutilation of her name. It wasn't that hard if you sounded it out. Of course, it sounded a little different in Ukrainian. Pavlenko was a pretty common surname in the country where her parents were born.

"Yes, I'm Alona Pavlenko."

"Mr. Oliver will see you now, ma'am. Please follow me."

Alona followed the woman down a long hallway with doors on either side. Stopping at a door midway, the woman gestured for her to enter. "In here please. Can I offer you coffee? Water?"

"No thank you," she answered automatically.

She entered the office and stopped dead as she saw the most attractive man she'd seen in real life sitting behind the desk. He was a white guy with light brown hair, cut a little shorter on the sides, and large almond-shaped eyes that were super blue. He was clean shaven with a square chin with one of those chin dimples she'd always loved. The man stood up, adjusting his suit jacket that did little to hide his athletic figure.

"Alona Pavlenko?" She noticed that he didn't hesitate over her last name. "Hi, I'm Jayden Oliver. Thanks for coming downtown to meet with me."

She almost laughed. Downtown was barely a ten-minute train ride from her office. Davis, Lang & White was donating considerable time and resources to this benefit. Alona would travel across the country if it helped her people.

He walked around the desk, reaching out to shake her hand. She caught a whiff of cologne as his large hand engulfed hers. She caught her breath as their skin touched, sending a little jolt of electricity up her arm. What was that?

"Nice to meet you," she said absently.

He was still holding her hand and giving her the oddest look. The air around them seemed to vibrate. Realizing that she was staring, she pulled away and took a deep breath.

"Shall we get to work?"

He gestured to a small table. Alona slipped into a chair at one side, Jayden sitting across from her.

"Before we get started, let's get this out of the way. Yes, I am *that* Jayden Oliver. That's why they asked me to work on this project, of course, for my connections."

She frowned in confusion. "That Jayden Oliver?"

"From the Oliver Boys."

She waited for him to say something else. When he didn't she frowned.

"I'm sorry Mr. Oliver, I don't understand what you mean."

He continued to watch her. "You know, Jayden from the Oliver Boys rock band?"

She shook her head. "I'm not sure what you're trying to tell me."

"You don't know who I am?" he asked.

Her frown deepened. This was one of the weirdest conversations she'd ever had.

"You're Jayden Oliver, you just introduced yourself. Are you okay Mr. Oliver? You're not making a lot of sense."

She was starting to wonder if this guy had a head injury. He leaned forward and gave her an unnerving stare.

"You really don't know who I am? Don't you listen to music?"

She nodded.

"And you don't know the Oliver Boys?"

She shook her head. "I guess it sounds vaguely familiar?"

"We were kind of a big deal."

"We?"

"Me and my brothers, the Oliver Boys. Our band sold millions of albums and were famous around the world. Got mobbed everywhere we went. We even played in Kyiv once. It was a full house, of course, but then again, we pretty much sold out every venue we played."

Was she supposed to be impressed by this? What an arrogant man. Knowing that he was a former musician did not exactly give her confidence in his ability to help shoulder the load of organizing this benefit concert. She hoped he wasn't going to expect her to do all the work.

"Anyway, as soon as we're done here I'll reach out to my brothers. We've been talking about doing a reunion show, and I think a benefit concert for Ukraine is a terrific opportunity for us to give our fans what they've been hoping for these last few years."

Why did it feel like they were having two different conversations?

"I thought you were an attorney here?"

"I am an attorney now," he confirmed. "But I was super famous before the band retired. The fans always loved me best." He winked.

"Good for you Mr. Oliver, but can we please focus on the matter at hand? I've only got an hour and we've got a lot of work to do to get this project off the ground."

For a moment he looked like she'd kicked his puppy or something, but then he smoothed his expression into what she could tell was a practiced smile.

"Very well then, let's get started. And please, call me Jayden."

She pulled out her laptop and opened her project management software. Trello was a lifesaver for her when she was planning events or working on complex projects.

"I'm going to invite you to my Trello board if that's okay, then we can both track tasks in here. Unless you have a project management software you prefer to use?"

"Nope. That sounds good, Alona."

How did he make her name sound like a caress? Jayden Oliver was way too attractive for his own good, and if there was one thing Alona hated, it was overconfident men. She'd dealt with a lot of them in her life, none of them good. As she keyed his email into the app to send him an access link for her Trello board she resolved to maintain her distance. She wasn't sure what it was about him, but one thing was clear: Jayden Oliver was trouble.

Jayden

Jayden watched Alona as she typed into her laptop. She was a stunner, all creamy white skin and sensuous curves. Long, straight brown hair fell to her shoulders, framing her lovely face. She had brown eyes bracketed by tiny laugh lines, a sharp nose that was just a little too big for her face, and the cutest little pink mouth. She didn't seem to be wearing make-up, other than a little lip gloss, not that she needed it. She was beautiful just as she was.

She was dressed conservatively in a black skirt and a black and white polka dot shirt, the top two buttons open and giving him a glimpse of her ample cleavage. She was the tiniest bit plump, and he had to say he liked it. He'd never been one who liked women who looked like they would break under a rough fucking.

Speaking of fucking, every time she frowned at him his dick twitched. Stern looked good on her.

He was surprised she didn't know about the band. Pretty much every woman in their age group loved the band, and most of them had a favorite brother they crushed on when they were teenagers. Maybe she was older than him and had missed all the fervor about the Oliver Boys? But even now they were on the radio all the time.

Based on her Chicago accent, she'd been raised here so that couldn't be the reason she didn't know who he was. He wondered if her parents were religious or something. He reminded himself that he *liked* it when people didn't fawn all over him or ask him about his supposedly glamorous lifestyle. He wasn't sure why it bothered him that she didn't seem to know that he'd been famous, but it did.

"What kind of music do you like?" he asked, even as he asked himself why he couldn't let this go.

She frowned again and he shifted in his chair. He'd be masturbating to that look later, he was sure of it.

"Eighties music, why?"

"What, like Cyndi Lauper and Madonna?"

She rolled her eyes like he was an idiot. "No. Like Depeche Mode. Erasure. New Order. Squeeze."

He nodded. "Ah, okay. Maybe we can get one of your favorites to play at the benefit. I'll put a call into my old agent."

She looked skeptical but typed into her laptop. "I'm adding it to the to-do list."

He wondered what it took to impress this Ukrainian beauty.

The next forty-five minutes passed quickly, with the two of them divvying up tasks and brainstorming about who to invite to their planning committee as well as potential locations for the concert.

"Okay then, I'll put a call into our board member and see if we can get access to the Chicago Music Hall," she said, referencing one of the many music venues in the city. "I understand it can hold a large crowd. Once we have the date and location locked in, we can move backwards from there. It would be really cool if we can get August twenty-fourth."

"Why August twenty-fourth?" he asked

"Because that's our Ukrainian Independence Day."

"Oh yeah, I love that idea. It would be a nice connection."

The conversation paused while Alona continued typing and then closed down her laptop. Desperate to learn more about her, he asked, "Do you mind if I ask, did you grow up here? I know you work at RUC, but your accent is all Chicago."

She gave him a faint smile. "Yeah my parents emigrated here in 1980, a couple of years before I was born. I grew up in Ukrainian Village," she said, referring to a neighborhood on Chicago's west side that was historically Ukrainian. "The neighborhood has gentrified significantly since then, but my folks still live there."

"I can't wait to meet them," he said, surprising them both.

"Um, yeah, okay," she said.

She looked up, meeting his eyes for a long moment. He felt a zing go through his body, and somewhere deep in his mind he heard the word "mine". Jayden almost gasped as he realized the truth: he was in love. He came from a long line of men who'd fallen in love at first sight, including his brothers, and he'd heard what this was like. He'd never really believed in love at first sight, despite what his family told him, but after less than an hour with Alona, he knew it was possible. Jayden Oliver had finally met "the one".

"When can I see you again?" he asked.

She gave him a strange look, and he rushed to add, "To work on the concert."

"Oh, um, I need to check my schedule."

He nodded, then grabbed his phone out of his pocket. "Why don't you give me your number so we can stay in touch?"

She looked hesitant but rattled off her number. Jayden input it into his phone, gave her the contact name "Future Wife", then texted her so she'd have his number too. He heard her phone vibrate from her bag, but she made no move to grab it.

"That's me," he said unnecessarily.

"I figured."

God, he was really off his game with her. He was usually charming and loquacious, it's what made him such a good lawyer. With Alona, he was bragging and bumbling like a teenager with his first crush. He was pretty sure he had better game in high school than he did with his co-chair.

"I guess I'll see you later, Alona."

She gave him another of those cryptic looks, then turned around to leave, calling "goodbye" as she strode out of his office. He watched her go, then collapsed back down in his chair, rubbing the sudden ache in his sternum. He'd finally met "the one". An hour ago, he would have scoffed at that, despite each of his four siblings finding the perfect partner. But now, now he knew. Today was the first day of the rest of his life, and that life would include Alona if it was the last thing he did.

Alona

Alona thumbed through google search links on her phone as she waited for the elevated train to come. "The El", as it was known to Chicago residents, connected the downtown core to the residential neighborhoods via train tracks that ran over the city in some parts. In a city where parking was a premium, the El was the easiest way to get around.

Her search for Jayden Oliver produced over a million hits. Frowning, she selected the Wikipedia page for him and read up on her concert planning co-chair. She hummed to herself as she realized it wasn't just conceit when Jayden said he was famous, he and his brothers had really been international superstars.

She'd never been one for pop culture. Her parents had snuck out of Ukraine to escape persecution during the Soviet era, and like many first-generation immigrants, they raised their kids to be well-versed in the culture of their home country. Somewhere along the way, she'd fallen in love with alternative music from the 1980s, and other than Ukrainian music, that was most of what she listened to.

As she skimmed the page, she vaguely remembered girls in college being excited about the band, but she'd been way too busy studying to worry about silly crushes on boy bands.

She clicked over to the band's Wikipedia page, noting that Jayden was the youngest brother out of four. They were all too good looking for their own good, but there was something about Jayden that caught her attention more than his brothers. He was thirty-five now, three years younger than she was and, according to the page, the only brother who was still single.

She tamped down a sense of relief at that. It shouldn't matter that he was single. She was *not* going to get a crush on her co-chair. It was bad enough that he had that confident swagger that she hated in a man, but he'd also clearly lived a life full of sex, drugs, and rock 'n roll. Maybe she was old-fashioned, but Alona believed in monogamy, family, and everything in moderation.

The way she'd reacted to him in his office had to be a fluke. It had been a while since she'd dated anyone, that must be why she had felt such an intense attraction to him. Maybe she should log into one of those dating apps on her phone and see if there were any good prospects for her.

She had just returned to her tiny condo on the west side when her phone vibrated with a text from Jayden.

Jayden: *Hey Alona it's Jayden. I just wanted to let you know that I talked to my brothers and they're in for an Oliver Boys reunion set at the concert.*

Alona: *OK, thanks*

Jayden: *We'll sell out the stadium for sure now.*

Alona: *OK*

Jayden: *What are you doing right now? Would you be up for dinner?*

She stared at the phone in confusion. What was he doing?

Alona: *We had a meeting two hours ago. I don't have any updates on the project, and since you just gave me yours, we should be good for now.*

Jayden: *I know, but I thought we could get to know each other over dinner. You're single, right? (praying hands emoji)*

Alona's mouth dropped open at his gall.

Alona: *Are you asking me on a date?*

Jayden: *Yes. How about it? Anywhere you want to go.*

Alona: *No thanks*

Jayden: *Why? Are you busy tonight?*

Alona: *I don't date people I work with.*

Jayden: *Technically we're both volunteering.*

Alona: *I don't date people I volunteer with either. Besides, you don't even know if I'm single.*

Jayden: *You weren't wearing a ring. Are you seeing someone that I need to steal you away from?*

Alona: *None of your business. Let's just keep things professional. I'll see you at our meeting next week.*

Jayden: *You wound me. How about a drink? It's shorter than dinner.*

Alona: *Goodbye*

As Alona made dinner, she wondered if she should have accepted Jayden's invitation. Reminding herself that his values were very different from hers did nothing to cool her fascination with him. It wasn't the first time she'd been around someone famous, so she knew it wasn't that she was starstruck. There was something about him that made her feel kind of hopeful, kind of attractive, and very lustful.

Her phone rang, drawing her out of her Jayden reverie. She smiled when she saw it was her mother.

"Hi Mama," she greeted her in their native Ukrainian language. "How are you? What's new?"

Knowing that question would occupy her mother for a while, Alona finished preparing her dinner. She listened as her mother give her updates on what was happening with various family members and neighbors. Her mother loved gossip.

"How is the benefit concert planning going?" her mother finally asked.

"It is going well, Mama. A law firm agreed to be our sponsor, and they assigned one of the attorneys to help me with planning. We are hoping to hold the event on Ukrainian Independence Day."

Her mother's voice turned sly with interest.

"A lawyer, huh? Is he single?"

Alona laughed. "Mama, you don't even know how old he is. Maybe he's seventy-five years old."

"Is he?"

"No, he's three years younger than me."

She bit her lip, hoping her mother didn't ask how she knew that. Sharing your ages wasn't typically something that happened in a business meeting.

"Three years is nothing at your age. Maybe you should ask him out. I would like it for you to marry a handsome young lawyer."

She rolled her eyes. "How do you know he's handsome?"

"You just told me," her mother said smugly.

Damn it. Her mother had always been sneaky. She could never get anything over on her.

"My dinner is ready Mama, I need to go before my meal gets cold," she said, grateful to have a reason to get off the phone.

"Don't stay single forever Alona, your eggs are drying up you know."

She rolled her eyes again, glad her mother couldn't see her.

"OK Mama, I've got to go. I love you."

"I love you as well Alona, that's why I don't want you to be alone."

"I'm not alone Mama, I have you and Tato and Olga."

"And someday you father and I will be dead," her mother reminded her pragmatically. "And what will you do then?"

She suppressed a sigh. "I guess I'll get a cat."

Jayden

His phone rang around nine o'clock that evening. Hoping it was Alona, he answered without checking the screen.

"This is Jayden."

"Hey little brother," his sister Jen greeted him. He bit back his disappointment. He knew there was no way Alona was going to call him yet, and he really loved talking to his big sister. Jen was the oldest of their siblings, and Jayden was the youngest, so they'd always had a special bond.

"I hear you're having a big concert to help Ukrainian refugees and didn't invite me. What's up with that?"

Jayden shook his head. The Oliver sibling grapevine worked fast.

"Who told you that?"

"Jim and Paige came for dinner tonight and told us about it," she explained. "And also, Justin texted me with the news. How come I wasn't included in this conversation?"

"I asked the guys to do a set for the concert."

"So?"

"You were never in the band, remember?"

"Yeah but you know I'm a genius at organizing things. I don't understand why I wouldn't have been your first call."

This was true. His sister was bossy and organized, a great combination for complex projects. Except for one problem...

"You live in Kansas."

"What difference does that make? I have the internet here you know, and a telephone too. You can send me assignments that I can work on from here. And Nick volunteered to help you with security."

His brother in law was the chief of security back when the band used to be together. But then he'd married their sister and moved to Kansas, opening a private security firm he could mostly manage from the family farm.

"That would be great, thanks." Jayden had been planning to ask him anyway, but it was easier for Nick to volunteer instead.

"We'll both come to Chicago for the show too. You know grandma was Ukrainian, so it's the least we can do."

"What about the kids?" he asked.

"We'll get a sitter for the weekend. Besides, it may be our last time to be alone for a while, and I could use a break."

Jayden immediately connected the dots. "Jesus Christ, did Nick knock you up again?"

Jen and Nick already had two kids under five. Clearly their former security chief and sister were very fertile.

"Yep. That's the other thing I called to tell you. We just got confirmation today that I'm pregnant."

"Wow. Well, congratulations. I hope we're not running out of J names."

It was a tradition in their family to give all the kids a name beginning with the letter J. No one knew how it had started, but his siblings had continued the tradition with their own kids.

"It's probably our last one. I'm not getting any younger. The doctor is already calling it a geriatric pregnancy and suggesting that I get my tubes tied," she huffed. "Can you believe that? I'm only in my early forties for cripe's sake."

"That's ridiculous."

He'd learned long ago not to argue with his sister when she was ranting. Or being bossy. Or talking at all, really. His sister took her job as the oldest very seriously, and never missed a chance to tell them how to live their lives. Speaking of which...he'd better tell her the news before his brothers heard about it.

"So, I met someone."

Jen squealed so loudly he grimaced. She'd been riding him to find someone to settle down with ever since he'd graduated law school two years ago.

"Really? What's her name? How did you meet her? How old is she? What does she do?"

Besides being a nag, his sister was also the nosiest person he knew, with impressive interrogation skills.

"Her name is Alona Pavlenko. She works for a Ukrainian refugee charity in the city. We're working together on the concert as co-chairs."

"Oh my God, what's she like?"

"She's beautiful," he said reverently. "Strong. Very smart."

"And?" his sister prompted, sensing his hesitation.

"She doesn't seem to like me very much."

His sister snorted. "Well, that's how Johnny and Janie started. Remember how she poured beer on him? And Jim and Paige had a rocky start, especially with her being his boss. Oh, and I guess Peggy wasn't super fond of Justin at first either, at least not the second time they met. I guess this is how relationships start for you boys. You're all like one of those enemies to lovers romance books."

"As I recall you weren't too impressed with Nick in the beginning either."

When Nick had first visited the family farm in Kansas with the guys, he and Jen had been like oil and water. Bossy versus bossy. The only time they weren't fighting was when they were loudly fucking. Thankfully, the guys were able to sleep in their touring bus during that visit.

Jen giggled. "Well, I got over that. Anyway, just keep showing up and being charming, and she'll come along. Falling in love with us Olivers is like boiling a frog."

"Huh?" he asked in confusion.

"You know how they put a frog in a pot of cold water, and they just keep increasing the temperature and the frog just gets used to being hot and doesn't realize that he's actually being boiled alive?"

"I don't think that analogy works for dating, Jenny."

"Of course it does," his sister retorted. "Just keep turning up the temperature around your Alona. She'll be cooked before you know it."

"And by cooked you mean?"

"Used to you."

"Yeah," he said drily, "That's my goal, to get Alona used to me."

"Have I ever steered you wrong with my advice Jay-Jay?"

"No."

"Okay then."

Jayden heard wailing in the background.

"Listen I gotta go see what my little rug rats are getting into. Nick is working tonight so I need to get them ready for bed. Email me some information tomorrow and I'll check in with you later."

She hung up before he could say goodbye. Typical Jen.

But as he replayed the conversation with his sister, Jayden realized that she had a good idea. He already knew that Alona was the woman for him, but if she needed more time to learn to love him, well, he'd give her more time. He was confident that if they could just get to know each other better Alona would see that they were meant to be. He just needed to figure out how to make that happen.

Alona

Alona paced back and forth on the sidewalk in front of the Chicago Music Hall, trying to tamp down her nerves. It had been almost a week since she'd met Jayden. He'd texted her every day, ostensibly about the concert, but always managed to veer into personal topics until she pulled him back. She had a feeling he wasn't used to being told "no" by a woman. She was clearly a challenge for him, but she had too much respect for herself to become one of his ridiculous music groupies.

She didn't want to be with some rich asshole who partied all night. She wanted a guy who was a partner, someone who shared her same values, someone who valued family and stability over money and partying.

"Alona, hey."

She jolted as Jayden's deep rumble sounded behind her. Turning, she took in his navy blue suit. It fit him like it was custom tailored, which it probably was. He'd paired it with a starched white dress suit and a geometric patterned tie that he'd loosened a bit. He looked like one of those guys on the cover of a billionaire romance, which made sense she guessed since he was actually a billionaire. She felt dowdy next to him in faded jeans, trainers, and a slim-fitting sweater which was perfect for Spring in Chicago, where there were often rapid temperature fluctuations.

"Hi Jayden." She greeted him with a polite smile. "Ready to go in and check out the site?"

She reached for the door, but he was faster, grabbing the edge just over her head.

"After you," he said gallantly.

She scooted under his arm and into the lobby where the theater manager was waiting for them. Rob was a good friend of one of her board members, and half Ukrainian himself. There was a large contingent of

Ukrainians in the Chicagoland area, and a lot of them knew each other socially or through their church.

"Alona! You're looking lovelier every time I see you," Rob said as he pulled her into a warm hug.

She heard what sounded like a low growl behind her.

"I'm Jayden Oliver," her co-chair said firmly, moving forward and forcing Rob to let her go to shake his hand. "It's nice to meet you."

"Great to meet you too, man. I'm a huge fan."

At Alona's raised eyebrows he amended, "Well, my older sister was obsessed with the band, so I was forced to listen to Oliver Boys music until I learned to love it. I couldn't tell my friends that though, didn't want to lose my man card."

Jayden chuckled at his honesty. Fans of boy bands like the Oliver Boys were almost always girls and young women.

"It's always nice to meet a fan, even if they're a secret fan. Shall we check out the space?"

Alona and Jayden trailed Rob as he showed them around, stopping from time to time to point something out. She'd been here before, but this time she was looking at the venue from a different perspective, trying to imagine how things would work for the concert. Meanwhile, Jayden was taking notes on his phone and asking questions she never would have thought about. Alona was impressed with how committed he seemed to the project. Despite his rock star history, he clearly was a hard worker with a sharp mind. Of course, he couldn't be a total idiot; he had passed the bar, which was no small task.

Rob's phone rang, the sound loud in the silence of the cavernous performance space. "I'm sorry, but I need to get this, I'll be right back. Feel free to keep looking around and I'll catch up with you when I'm done."

Alona trailed Jayden as he examined the backstage area, leading her to a long hallway.

"The dressing rooms will be back here."

She followed behind him as he opened a door, realizing too late that the room was a janitor's closet. The door closed behind them automatically. She looked around at the mop heads, toilet paper, and cleaning products and laughed.

"I always thought dressing rooms would be fancier."

Jayden turned with a smile, and she realized that they were somehow very close to each other in a confined space. Their eyes met, and the space instantly heated up. Only a few inches from him, Alona could feel the heat coming off his body in waves.

"Um...," she trailed off, at a loss for words.

God, what was that cologne he wore? She wanted to bathe in it. She could feel her core throbbing just from the seductive look he was giving her, a look that said he wanted to do dirty things to her.

Jayden moved half a step closer, and she instinctively stepped back, still staring into his blue eyes. Another step forward, another step back, and suddenly her back was pressed against the door. She felt a trickle of sweat move down her back as the small space heated up, although she couldn't say whether it was from their body heat or the attraction shimmering between them. Her heart was pounding so hard she could hear it in her ears.

"Alona," he whispered, his voice rough.

Slowly, deliberately, he placed his palms against the door on either side of her head, trapping Alona between him and the door. It should have made her uncomfortable, but it only ratcheted up her arousal. She pressed her thighs together as she felt her panties dampen. She felt herself sway slightly towards him and he immediately shifted forward, closing the small distance between them, and pressing his lips against hers.

The minute their lips touched, it was like everything inside her calmed and got excited all at once. His lips were soft but firm, and Alona pressed her head back against the door as he deepened the kiss. She opened for his exploring tongue and gasped at the flood of sensations coursing through her body. The man really knew how to kiss. She forgot why that was a bad thing.

Jayden slipped his hands around her waist and down to the lush curve of her ass, pulling them closer to each other. His growing erection pressed against her stomach, heightening her excitement. She responded by sliding her hands underneath his suit coat to explore the muscles of his back through the fabric of his dress shirt. He felt surprisingly fit for someone with a desk job.

"Alona? Jayden? Are you back here?"

She gave Jayden a hard shove back as Rob's voice penetrated the haze. "Fuck," she hissed, wiping her mouth with the back of her hand. "What was that?"

Jayden smoothed down his shirt and gave her a cocky smirk, as if he could tell how much of an effect he was having on her and was quite pleased about it.

"If you don't know what that was, you clearly need to be kissed more thoroughly. And more often."

She rolled her eyes and wrenched the door open, hurrying out of the closet. She willed her racing heart to slow down as she walked quickly towards the stage area, assuming that Rob had headed back there. Jayden stayed behind in the closet, waiting for his hard-on to subside, she suspected. She silently berated herself for letting him kiss her, for losing control, for acting so unprofessional. Making out with a virtual stranger wasn't like her, not at all.

One thing was clear: she needed to keep as much distance between herself and Jayden as she could before things went farther than she wanted.

Jayden

Jayden rested his forehead against the closet door, breathing deeply and willing his hard-on to go down. Holy crap. He hadn't intended to kiss Alona, but he didn't regret it either. He'd seen the look of shock on her beautiful face as she practically sprinted from the closet. She was as impacted by this attraction between them as he was. If he'd had any doubts, they were gone now.

He just needed to figure out his next steps with her.

He found Alona and Rob standing on the stage, looking out over the rows of seats, and talking quietly. If he closed his eyes, he could imagine being up there, playing music and hamming it up with his brothers as they'd done for so many years.

"This space is perfect."

Alona nodded in agreement. "Do you have a contract for us to look over, Rob?"

The venue manager slid a packet of stapled papers off of his clipboard and handed them to Alona, who handed them to Jayden.

"I'll just have my attorney look these over," she joked.

Rob smiled at her with more familiarity than Jayden felt comfortable with.

"Listen I've got to get to my next appointment soon, but I'd love to grab a drink soon and catch up."

"Absolutely. I'd love to catch up. Tell your mama I said hello."

Alona moved in to give Rob a hug, and Jayden visualized himself ripping her out of Rob's arms and punching the guy in the face. He was vaguely disturbed by the thought; he'd never hit anyone in his life. Other than his brothers, of course. He was the easy-going brother. The pacifist. But that all flew out the window when it came to his woman. And she was his, whether she knew it or not.

As they walked out of the theater, Jayden touched her arm.

"How about dinner?"

She avoided his gaze. "I don't think that's a good idea."

"Please?"

She looked up at him, her brow wrinkled in confusion. "If this is about what happened in the utility closet, it was a mistake."

"No, it wasn't. I've wanted to do that since the first time I saw you. And I think you did too."

She opened her mouth to object, and he held up his hand.

"Let's just have dinner and get to know each other. Just dinner. We're going to be working together closely for the next six weeks until the concert, why not be friends?"

She looked a bit suspicious. He didn't blame her. He didn't want to be her friend. Well, he did want to be her friend, but he also wanted to be something more. But he could tell she doubted his intentions. He didn't even blame her. She'd likely heard some of the wild things he'd done when he was a rock star. Some of the stories were exaggerated of course, but there was enough truth in them that he was ashamed of how he'd behaved for so long. His grandparents had raised him and his brothers better. They'd forgotten that for a long time, their heads turned around by fame and constant adoration. In the end, they retired at the height of their fame to get away from it all.

"Okay, we can have dinner," she said. "Just dinner."

Jayden released a breath he didn't even know he was holding.

"But no touching. Business only."

She pointed her finger at him and gave him a stern look that had his cock twitching again. He took a deep breath and willed it to relax.

"And nothing fancy, I'm not dressed for fancy."

"Got it. I know just the place. Let's go."

Twenty minutes later they were holed up in a corner booth at a cute little restaurant not far from his office. It was a family-run place with a huge menu and plain but delicious food, exactly the kind of place they had back in Kansas. It had high-backed booths, stained glass lamps hanging over the tables, and a simple but delicious menu. It was a bit out of place amongst the fancier dining options in downtown Chicago, which made him love it even more.

They both ordered a beer, and Alona looked around curiously, obviously surprised at his selection.

"Something wrong?"

She shook her head and gave him a small smile. "No, not at all. I just didn't expect you to know about a place like this. This is more of a working class place, not a billionaire rock star lawyer kind of place."

"Actually, I come here all the time. It reminds me of home."

She tilted her head curiously. "Where's home?"

"I grew up on a farm in a small town in Kansas."

"Wow. I assumed someone like you probably grew up in L.A. or something."

He smirked. "I hate L.A. We lived there for over ten years between tours, but it never felt like home."

"And does Chicago feel like home?"

He gave her a heated look. "It does now."

The waitress came by, interrupting them. She slid their beers on the table, then took their food orders. Jayden ordered a cheeseburger and fries, and Alona ordered the fried chicken.

"You won't be sorry," he told her after the waitress rushed away. "Their chicken is delicious."

She nodded but didn't respond.

"Tell me about yourself, Alona."

She gave him a look Jayden couldn't interpret.

"There's not much to say," she started, looking a little uncomfortable. "I was born and raised here in Chicago, went to DePaul for college, and eventually wound up at RUC."

"I went to DePaul for undergrad too. What did you major in?" he asked.

"Hospitality Management," she said. "I worked at a couple of hotels downtown and realized that I had a knack for events planning. Eventually I got hired on at RUC doing fundraising and events there."

"Do you like it?"

She looked thoughtful. She always seemed to choose her words carefully.

"Yeah, I do," she finally responded. "I like being able to use my skills to help people like my parents. Being an immigrant is a hard transition. It's such a different world in the U.S. You've done a lot of traveling..."

He nodded.

"So, you can probably understand how overwhelming it might be to come from a country where everyone is so poor and practical and then people get here and it's...like being on a different planet. Everything is bigger and kind of excessive. Even the basic things you do every day are different. My mother always tells the story about the first time they went grocery shopping here. Coming from the Soviet bloc, they were used to having only one or two options in the store for any product. Not long after they arrived, they walked into the Jewel, and the first aisle they walked down was the cereal aisle. They were so overwhelmed by all the shelves and shelves of choices, they kind of freaked out and had to leave. And of course, they had to deal with a lot of bias here about being foreigners, having accents, that kind of thing."

"Are you close with your parents?"

"Yes, we've always been tight, my parents and my little sister and me. How about you?"

"My parents died when I was just a baby. Car accident."

She let out a tiny gasp. "Oh, wow, I'm sorry. I didn't know. That's awful."

He shrugged. "I don't remember them at all, but it was harder on my older siblings for sure. When my parents died, we went to live on the family farm with my grandparents. It was hard work, and we never had a lot of money, but my grandparents loved us and took care of us all. We had a great childhood because of them."

"How many siblings do you have?" she asked curiously.

"Four."

Her eyes widened but she didn't comment.

"My sister Jen is the oldest, then there's Johnny, Justin, Jim, and me."

"You guys like the letter J?"

Jayden laughed. "Yeah, and my siblings have continued the tradition with their own kids."

"Was your sister in the band too?" she asked.

"Naw, she always hated the band, especially after we got famous. We started to believe our own publicity, and basically forgot how we were raised. We were drinking and partying and acting like assholes. It created an estrangement with my sister for a while, especially after our grandparents died. We were on tour at the time, and we couldn't get out of our shows to attend the funeral. Jen was furious with us."

"And now?"

"Now we're all thick as thieves again. We stopped performing five years ago now, and during that time every single one of my siblings has found their person and fallen in love. They're all married now, everyone except for me."

"No one trapped you into marriage yet?" she teased.

He met and held her gaze, the connection between them almost vibrating.

"Us Olivers believe marriage is a lifetime commitment. I've never even considered marriage. Until now."

Alona

She looked at Jayden and felt annoyance bubbling up. He wanted to marry someone? He'd just had his tongue down her throat not thirty minutes ago.

"You have a girlfriend and you kissed me?" she whisper-shouted.

Jayden reached across the table and grabbed her hand. His larger hand completely engulfed hers, sending currents of electricity right to her core. His fingers were calloused, and she wondered idly if it was from all those years playing the guitar.

"I don't have a girlfriend," he responded carefully. "I would never have touched you if I did. Here's another thing to know about us Olivers. We fall in love at first sight, and we fall hard."

She frowned, unsure what he was getting at.

"Um. Okay. But that doesn't explain what happened between us in the closet."

God, she hoped he could explain the kiss, because she sure as hell couldn't. She'd never made out with a near stranger in her life, and certainly never in a utility closet. It was like once she was alone with him in a confined space, all of her inhibitions went out the window. He was too damn attractive.

His hand tightened around hers. "I'm declaring my intentions Alona. I knew the minute I saw you that you were meant to be mine."

"What?"

Her heart stopped for a long moment, then restarted with a jolt. She pulled her hand away and tucked it under her thigh for good measure, making sure she didn't reach for him again. Jayden opened his mouth to respond but the waitress came, interrupting them. He waited until she'd set the food down and left the table before he spoke again.

"I'm saying I have feelings for you, Alona. I know it sounds crazy, but when I met you last week I knew: you're the one I've been waiting for my whole life."

She picked up a piece of chicken and ripped off a bite, chewing slowly to give herself time to respond.

"Did you do a lot of drugs when you were a rock star?' she finally asked. It was the only logical explanation.

He looked confused.

"No, I've never done drugs in my life. Except for smoking pot, but everybody does that. Why?"

"I'm just trying to figure out if you have brain damage or something."

"I don't have brain damage," he said.

"Then you're either completely insane, or you're messing with me. Either way, I don't want any part of this. There's no such thing as love at first sight."

She started sliding out of the booth, intending to get the hell out there, but Jayden stopped her by sliding his foot up on the seat next to her. The guy had long legs.

"Please don't go. I hear that you're not where I'm at yet, and I get that. I'm not trying to pressure you, but can't you please just give me a chance? Give us a chance? Let's just spend some time together and get to know each other better."

She shook her head.

"I'm not interested." She looked pointedly at his foot on the bench next to her. "Now if you don't mind, please move your foot. I really need to go home."

He looked wounded, almost like she'd hurt his feelings. It made her chest ache, but she kept her expression firm. After a long moment, he moved his foot, allowing her to leave the booth.

"At least take your dinner with you," he said. "We can get a to-go box."

"I'm not hungry anymore. Goodbye."

She rushed out of the restaurant and practically ran to the El station. Thankfully, the train pulled up to the platform as soon as she reached the top of the steps. She slid in and collapsed on a seat, breathing heavily.

What the hell had just happened? She'd made out with a near stranger in a closet, and then he told her that they were somehow fated to be together. How was this her life?

When she came into work the next day, there was an enormous bouquet of flowers on her desk. Colorful wildflowers were interspersed with greenery. It was beautiful.

"What's this?" she asked Ana, the assistant that she and her co-workers all shared.

"Flowers, I think."

Alona rolled her eyes at the sarcastic response. "Obviously. Where did they come from?"

"I have no idea. I'd suggest you read the card."

She examined the flowers carefully, as if something was going to pop out at her. They were a beautiful collection of colorful wildflowers, interspersed with greenery. She slid the card out of the plastic holder, confirming that "Alona Pavlenko" was written neatly on the envelope. She opened the flap and slid out the card.

Alona, I'm sorry if I freaked you out yesterday by coming on too strong, but I want you to know I meant everything I said. Can we go out tonight? Please give me a chance to get to know you better. Thinking of you, Jayden

She crumpled up the card and tossed it into the trash, then took the flowers to the employee break room and placed them on the long table where people ate lunch. It certainly brightened up the dull space. They were a relatively small organization, and they couldn't afford luxuries like matching furniture or paint that hadn't been there since before she was born.

She stalked back to her desk, lost in thought. Thinking about Jayden had kept her up all night, and she was not happy about it. Not at all. She wasn't sure what game Jayden was playing, but she wanted no part of it.

The next morning, he texted her just before nine.

Jayden: *Did you get the flowers?*

Alona: *Yes.*

Alona: *Thank you.*
Jayden: *Can we meet for lunch today?*
Alona: *No*
Jayden*: Why not?*
Alona: *I'm too busy to play games with you.*
Jayden: *I'm not playing games. I meant everything I said. Give me a chance to prove it to you.*
Alona: *I'll see you at our next planning meeting. There's no reason to talk before then.*

She watched the bubbles appear and disappear, until they finally stopped. She felt a stab of disappointment, then reminded herself that he was clearly a player, and way too charming for his own good. Still, she was surprised he gave up so soon.

A couple hours later Ana stuck her head in her office, looking excited.

"Come to the lunchroom. Someone sent lunch for the whole team."

Alona's eyes widened in surprise. "What? Who would do that?"

"Someone you know, I guess. Come check it out."

Alona followed Ana into the lunchroom where her coworkers were milling around with the excitement of kids who just found out they got a snow day. None of them made a lot of money since they were working at a nonprofit, and on the rare occasion they got free food, people descended like vultures. The table was practically groaning with a selection of food, including several types of meat, vegetables, salads, bread, and dessert. A cooler under the table was filled with sodas and cans of sparkling water. As soon as she entered, every person in the room turned to give her a curious look.

Alona looked around. "What? What's going on?"

"There's a card for you, Alona," Ana said, pointing out an envelope propped up against a serving tray of rice. Her name was written on the card in large block letters. "It came with the food."

She walked over, already knowing who it was from. There was only one person she knew who could afford to do something this extravagant. Although she couldn't be mad, not when she saw how excited her coworkers were about their free lunch.

Alona,

Since you don't have time for lunch today, I sent lunch to you. Please share with your coworkers. I hope you all enjoy it. You deserve a nice meal for all the great work you do at RUC.

Jayden

PS: This isn't a game. Not to me.

She looked up to find all of her coworkers watching her. She felt a flush rise up her neck and onto her cheeks.

"Is it the same guy who sent the flowers?" Ana asked.

"Yeah."

"He must be rich to send all this, and from one of the nicest restaurants in the city."

Alona waved her hand at the food.

"What are you guys waiting for? Eat. There's enough food here to feed an army."

Her coworkers hurried to get in line to load up their plates while Alona returned to her office. She laid her head on her desk with a long sigh. What was she going to do about this guy?

Jayden

Other than a terse text thanking him for sending lunch for her team, Alona didn't contact him for the rest of the day. He'd spent the afternoon staring at his phone like a lovelorn teen. He was tempted to contact her or go over to her house but decided to give her some time. The last thing he wanted was to push her away even more than he already had.

He worked late and fell asleep exhausted. His dreams were filled with Alona, and he woke up as hard as a rock. Foregoing the shower, he decided to go for a nice long run. He'd gotten into running when the band was touring; it was a great way to keep in shape and have some precious alone time, even if he usually had a bodyguard trailing him while he ran.

Leaving his townhouse, Jayden headed over to the multi-use path that ran along Lake Michigan. It was a lovely Saturday morning, and the path was crowded with runners, walkers, and bikers.

As he ran along the path, he daydreamed about Alona. Ever since his siblings had settled down, he'd wondered if he would ever meet anyone. He hadn't dated too much since he left the band. Going to college and law school had taken most of his time, and since he'd joined the firm he'd been working hard to meet his billable hours so he could prove himself. The truth was, he hadn't really met anyone he was interested in seeing more than once. Until he met Alona.

He'd spent his adult life surrounded by women who only wanted to be with him so they could brag about being with a celebrity. Women who only cared about his money and his connections. But Alona wasn't like that at all. His celebrity seemed to be a point against him, not the draw it was to other women.

Alona. She was perfect for him. She was smart, and dedicated to her work, and had a dry sense of humor that he appreciated. She was also...walking towards him.

He rubbed his eyes, wondering if he was hallucinating, but no, there she was. She was dressed in tight fitting capris and a tank top, with a jacket tied around her waist. An older woman walked on one side of her, and a younger woman on the other. He knew instantly that her companions were her mother and sister; the family resemblance was uncanny. He picked up his pace.

"Alona! Hey!"

She looked up, startled. Her eyes darted frantically between her mother and sister, and he could tell she was hoping he would just run past them and not stop. She hoped wrong. There was no way he'd let this opportunity go.

"What a coincidence running into you here," he said cheerfully as he stopped and pulled her into a hug.

She stood stiffly in his embrace, shooting him a glare. He stepped back and gave her mother his best "I'm a good guy" smile.

"You must be Alona's mother. I'm Jayden. It's so nice to meet you Mrs. Pavlenko."

The older woman shook his hand, looking between them speculatively. Her sister moved in front of Alona.

"Hi, I'm Olga, Alona's sister"

"Jayden Oliver," he said. "Nice to meet you."

"Jayden Oliver?" Olga asked, giving him a curious look. "Weren't you in that boy band?"

"The Oliver Boys, yes I was," he answered, shooting Alona a pointed look. "But now I'm a lawyer."

Mrs. Pavlenko gave Alona a significant look. "This is the lawyer you're working with?"

Jayden shot Alona a wink. "Have you been talking about me, beautiful?"

Alona's face flushed but she rolled her eyes. "Okay, well, it was nice seeing you Jayden, but we've got to go now. Bye."

Mrs. Pavlenko sent her a chastising look. "Don't be rude Alona. Maybe Mr. Oliver would like to join us for brunch."

Alona opened her mouth to argue, but he cut right in.

"I'd love to have brunch, and please, call me Jayden."

Jayden fell in line with them, his arm rubbing against Alona's with every step. It was definitely not on purpose.

A little while later they were waiting to be seated at a popular brunch restaurant in Lincoln Park. They'd been waiting about five minutes when one of the waitresses walked by them and did a double take.

"Are you Jayden Oliver?" she asked.

He nodded. "I am."

"Oh my God, I have to tell my mom, she's your biggest fan."

She rushed off and returned with an older woman who was wearing a name tag that said, "Susan, Manager". Jayden greeted Susan, answering her questions about the band, and giving her an autograph. He sent Alona a smug smile when Susan pulled them to the front of the line.

"Our VIP table is ready for you now, Mr. Oliver."

"We can wait our turn," Alona said stubbornly, glancing at the line.

Her mother shot her a glare, then wrapped her hand around Jayden's arm. "We'd love that ma'am, thank you."

Susan led them to a booth. Alona slid in one side, gesturing for her sister to sit next to her. Olga ignored her, sliding in the booth with her mother and leaving the seat next to Alona for Jayden. He sent Olga a grateful smile and slid in close, pressing his leg against Alona's. She studiously ignored him. He wondered if she felt the tingle of awareness everywhere they touched, the way he did.

Once they were seated and had ordered brunch from the overly solicitous server, Mrs. Pavlenko started quizzing him. He smiled internally, thinking that she would get along well with his sister Jen.

"You are a lawyer, yes?" she asked in her thick Ukrainian accent.

"Yes. I mostly practice environmental law."

Mrs. Pavlenko nodded approvingly.

"This is good. You are using your law degree to help people and save the environment, correct?"

"Yes I am."

"And you used to be a singer?"

"Yes, my brothers and I had a band. We were extremely popular for about twelve years. We traveled all over the world."

"You were a wild one, no? Making parties like the stories I see in the People magazine?"

He nodded.

"I'm not going to lie to you, there was a long time when my brothers and I were pretty wild. It's very easy to get turned around when you're surrounded by people telling you how great you are all the time. You start to believe your own P.R."

"And are you turned back around now?" she asked.

"I am. We all stopped drinking and partying after our grandparents died. It hit us all pretty hard. We left the music industry so we could live normal lives, the way our grandparents raised us. We were fortunate to make enough money to be comfortable with any life we chose."

"You invested your money?"

"Yes ma'am."

"Good boy."

Mrs. Pavlenko continued to pepper him with questions about his family and his job as they ate, while Alona and Olga were mostly silent. They were just finishing up their meals when Alona's mother turned the subject to her daughter.

"Now you are working with my Alona?"

"Yes, we are co-chairing the benefit concert for Ukraine."

"Those damn Russians," Olga said sadly. "They are destroying our country."

"As they have before," Mrs. Pavlenko said pragmatically. "We will prevail, as we always do. We all pray that good will triumph over evil. Slava Ukraini."

She took a deep breath, then turned back to him.

"Now onto happier topics. Jayden, my Alona is beautiful, is she not?"

He nodded emphatically. "She certainly is. I can tell she takes after her mother."

"Mama," Alona hissed.

Her mother ignored her warning, her sharp gaze watching Jayden carefully.

"Maybe you would like to take my Alona on a date? She has no husband or boyfriend. It is not good for a woman to be alone all the time."

"I would love to," he responded with his most earnest look. "But she keeps telling me no."

Alona's head whipped around so quickly he was worried she would get whiplash. She gave him a glare that made his dick twitch. He subtly dropped his hand to her thigh, feeling her muscles tighten and then relax beneath his hand. He used every ounce of restraint to keep his hand where it was and not move it any higher.

"Jayden is a nice young man, and a lawyer," Mrs. Pavlenko pointed out. "Why would you deny him?"

Alona sighed loudly. "Mama, I'm thirty-eight years old. I don't need your help with my dating life."

"Clearly you do," her mother said dismissively. "You are alone, what do they call it? Ah yes, you are an old maid. You don't care about the grandchildren I want to have."

Her gaze softened as she turned to Jayden. "What are you doing tomorrow young man?"

"Nothing important."

"Alona is free as well. You will take her out on a date tomorrow."

"No, I'm not free," Alona protested.

"When we were walking earlier you said you had nothing to do this weekend," Olga piped in helpfully, earning her a glare from her older sister.

"No, I said I was looking forward to relaxing, doing my laundry, and watching some Netflix."

Jayden bit his lip to keep himself from making a "Netflix and chill" joke.

Her mother made a dismissive gesture.

"It will be a beautiful day tomorrow, you will go out and have fun before your ovaries shrivel up."

Alona choked on her own spit as Olga burst out laughing. Mrs. Pavlenko set her fork down and gave them both a stubborn look, pointing first at Alona and then at Jayden.

"Do not disappoint me."

Alona

Alona spent the entire train ride home reliving the humiliation of her mother setting up a date for her. Damn Jayden Oliver for being so charming with her family. He'd even picked up the tab for everyone's brunch, despite her objections. She needed to put a stop to this dating nonsense right away. There was no way she wanted to date someone who didn't share her values.

She'd forgotten her phone at home, so as soon as she got home she texted Jayden.

Alona: *We don't need to do anything tomorrow.*

Jayden: *Yes we do. I want to see you, but even if I didn't, I'm scared of your mother. She looks like the type that would hit me with a wooden spoon if I don't take you out.*

Alona: *LOL. Well, that's true. But I really don't want to date right now.*

Jayden: *You don't want to date, or you don't want to date me?*

Alona: *Neither.*

Jayden: *Are you saying you are not attracted to me? Even after what happened in the closet?*

She stared at her phone, trying to decide how to respond. Hearing a knock on her door, she dropped her phone on the couch and opened the door, assuming it was her neighbor. She reared back in shock when she saw Jayden standing in the doorway, still wearing his running clothes, his phone in his hand. He looked like a model for a sportswear brand with his ruffled hair and super fit body.

"Hi."

"How did you know where I live?" she asked suspiciously.

"After you ran off to catch the El, I shared an Uber with your mom."

"My mother doesn't know how to use Uber."

"She does now. I dropped her off and she was kind enough to give me directions to your house and suggest I stop by and get an early start to our date."

Alona lived only about three miles away from her parents. She'd always appreciated being close to them, but now she wasn't too sure.

"Can I come in?"

She stepped back with a sigh. "I guess so."

Jayden looked around her small apartment curiously, taking in her comfortable furniture, family photos, and the large assortment of plants that filled every windowsill. She tried to see it from his perspective. She supposed her home looked pretty small and shabby to a guy who was a billionaire. He probably lived in a mansion in Lake Forest or one of the other rich people suburbs.

"Have a green thumb?" he asked.

She shrugged. "I guess. Why are you here, exactly?"

He looked uncharacteristically vulnerable.

"I don't know. Your mother gave me your address and I just came over without thinking, hoping that we could hang out or something."

Feeling bad about her churlishness, she plopped herself on the couch and gestured for him to join her.

"I was just going to watch a movie. Do you want to join me?"

His smile lit up her whole apartment and she felt a thrill at pleasing him. "Sure. That sounds perfect."

He sat down on the other side of the couch, leaving an empty cushion between them as she dug the remote out of the drawer and turned on the television.

"Have you seen the newest Marvel movie?" she asked, scanning her Netflix queue. "I've had it on my watch list."

"You like superhero movies?" he asked delightedly.

"Yeah, Olga and I have watched pretty much all of them I think."

"I knew it," he crowed.

"What?"

"You really are the woman of my dreams."

She rolled her eyes. "Let's just watch the movie and dial back the charm, okay?"

Several hours later, she awoke with a start. The living room was dark, other than the light from the screen saver on the television. She frowned as she realized that she and Jayden were wrapped around each other like pretzels. She reviewed the afternoon in her mind.

Jayden had come over unexpectedly and they'd watched a movie. Then she'd made popcorn and they wound up sitting close to each other on the couch, sharing a bowl while they watched a second movie in the series. At some point Jayden had dozed off and somehow slid down to rest his head on her lap. She may have stroked his soft hair while he slept, but she wasn't going to admit that to anyone besides herself. Now here she was with Jayden sprawled over her, his head on her stomach, their legs entwined. And she had a very pressing physical need to take care of.

Jayden's arm tightened around her torso as she started to slip out from under him. "Don't move," he whispered sleepily.

She pushed him gently. "I have to pee, and your head is pressing against my bladder."

He groaned and rolled over, freeing her to stand up. She hurried to the bathroom to take care of her business, and when she returned, Jayden was standing by the window, staring out into the street. When he heard her, he turned around and rubbed his stomach.

"You wanna order a pizza? I'm starving."

She tried not to notice how adorable he was, all sleepy and rumpled. "Sure. I'll call the place up the street. Any requests?"

"Naw, I eat anything."

"Anchovies and pineapple it is," she teased.

"You joke, but I like both of those things. I really do eat anything."

She made quick work of ordering a pizza while Jayden used the restroom. She skipped the anchovies and pineapple and ordered mushroom and sausage instead.

"Thirty minutes," she told Jayden as he came back to the living room.

He didn't respond. He had a look on his face that could only be described as feral. He stalked up to her, stopping only when they were about two inches apart. She resisted the urge to step back. Jayden reached up and tucked some of her hair behind her ear.

"I liked waking up with you," he said quietly.

His hand slid from her hair to cup the side of her face. Her brain was begging her to step away but her body, well, her body was suggesting that she climb him like a tree.

"Jayden..."

His eyes turned tender, almost like he could read her inner turmoil. He paused, giving her time to pull away, and when she didn't, he slowly lowered his head towards hers. She couldn't have stopped him for all the money in the world. Their kiss in the theater had been so hot that she'd been replaying it in her head for days and dreaming about it at night. She wanted, no needed to know, if it was just a fluke. She knew the minute their lips touched that it had been no fluke.

His lips were soft and gentle against hers. She made a noise in the back of her throat and stepped forward, eliminating the distance between them. His other hand came up to cup her other cheek as she slid her arms around his waist. Jayden licked along the seam of her mouth, and she willingly opened for him. Their tongues slid against each other, slowly exploring.

As the kiss went on, Jayden walked her backwards. When the back of her knees hit the edge of the couch he broke the kiss, and somehow managed to maneuver them so she was laying lengthwise on the cushion, with him stretched out on top of her.

"How did you do that?" she asked breathlessly.

"I've got skills," he winked at her before lowering his mouth to hers once more.

She gave herself up to the kiss, sliding her fingers into his short hair and tilting her pelvis until his impressive hard-on was notched against her in just the right position. He pumped against her, making her already damp panties totally soaked with her arousal. She hadn't dry humped a guy since her high school boyfriend, but she didn't remember it being so arousing. Of course, Jayden was way more experienced than Artem had been.

They broke away, panting for breath. Jayden shifted so his weight was on the side of her, then reached down to cup her breast. She was more than a handful, and he squeezed and stroked her until her nipple was tightened painfully against the fabric of her bra. Meanwhile, he peppered small kisses down the side of her neck and over her collarbone.

"You're so beautiful," he whispered, his mouth returning to hers in a kiss that made her see stars. She dug her fingers into his shoulders and shamelessly pumped her hips up against him. God, she was already so close...

A knock on the door startled them both.

"That's the pizza," she whispered.

Jayden levered off of her and headed towards the door, reaching for his wallet. Alona followed him.

"I already paid," she told him as he opened the door.

She greeted the kid holding the pizza. "Hey Jaymie, thanks for delivering that so fast."

"Anything for you, Alona," the boy smiled, a flush rising up his face. He nodded towards Jayden. "Everything okay here?"

She suppressed a smile. "Yeah, we're good, thank you."

Jaymie handed the pizza to Jayden with another suspicious look. "Let us know if you need anything else."

"Thanks Jaymie."

She closed the door and dropped the pizza onto her small dining room table, heading towards the kitchen with Jayden right behind her. It was a tiny space and she tried to avoid touching him lest she throw him onto the counter and start riding him. She didn't understand how their second kiss had been even hotter than the first one. If the pizza hadn't come when it did, she might have started begging him to fuck her. Then again, was that such a bad idea? Maybe if she gave in and had sex with him, it would get whatever this was out of her system, and things could go back to a normal, non-kissing working relationship.

"What would you like to drink?" she asked. "I have soda, sparkling water, regular water, or beer."

"Just a coke would be good," Jayden replied. "Where are the plates?"

She pointed towards the cabinet and got their drinks from the refrigerator. They sat down at the table, and she slid a couple of squares of pizza onto her plate. Looking up, she met Jayden's gaze and decided just this once, she was going to do something reckless, something just for herself.

"Do you want to stay over?"

Jayden

Jayden choked on the bite of pizza in his mouth. Was he hallucinating? He could have sworn she just asked him to stay over.

"Really?" he asked. He could hear the shock in his voice.

She nodded, looking resolved. Her hair was a tangle around her beautiful heart-shaped face, and he could see faint redness on her skin from where his stubble had rubbed against her face when they'd kissed.

She took a bite of pizza and chewed it slowly before adding, "I'm not normally one for casual sex but...well, I can't stop thinking about you since we kissed in the closet. And we're both single, so why not get it out of our systems?"

"Make no mistake Alona, there will be nothing casual about this."

A brief flash of fear lit her face, closely followed by irritation. "If we do this Jayden, it's one night. That's all I want."

"What if one night isn't enough to get it out of our systems?" he asked, knowing full well there was no way he could stop after one night with her.

One night would never be enough. He wasn't going to pretend otherwise, no matter how much he wanted her. A thousand nights would not be enough. He could tell by her expression that she knew that would be true as much as he did, as much as she was determined to ignore it.

"Then I guess we'll renegotiate."

He surged to standing and pulled her out of her chair and into his arms, holding her bridal style.

"Jayden! You're going to hurt yourself," she protested. "I'm a big girl."

"Where's the bedroom?"

"End of the hall."

He strode down the hallway, ignoring her protests about her being too heavy. When they reached the single bedroom, he gently set her down. He looked around, taking in the room. It was warm and comfortable. It had the requisite white walls that every apartment seemed to have, but she'd warmed up the space with beautiful artwork and tapestries. A queen sized bed took up most of the space, covered in a dark green comforter and a bunch of throw pillows. A matching green chair was in the corner next to a small table with a haphazard stack of books on it. A floor lamp sat behind the chair. More plants were lined along the window.

Reaching behind his head, he pulled off his shirt. Her eyes widened as she took in the muscled planes of his chest and abdomen. He might be in his mid-thirties, but he was committed to maintaining his exercise routine. All those years of working with a personal trainer had really paid off.

"Take off your clothes," he ordered, making his voice deeper.

Alona sent him a challenging look but pulled off her tank top and bra.

"You're kind of bossy, aren't you?" she asked.

He didn't answer, hypnotized by the sight of her full breasts. They were heavy and cream colored, a few shades lighter than the skin on her face and neck. Her areolas were dark red, and her nipples were hard and pointed right in his direction. At that moment, he wanted nothing more than to come on her beautiful breasts.

"You're a boob man, huh?" she asked wryly, as he continued to stare.

"I am now."

He shoved his running pants and briefs down, freeing his cock. It bounced up against his stomach and it was Alona's turn to stare. Jayden moved closer, falling to his knees in front of her as he pulled her capris and panties down to her ankles. He tapped her leg, and she stepped out, kicking her clothing out of the way. Wrapping his hands around the back of her thick thighs, he leaned forward to look at her neatly groomed pussy. He used his fingers to separate her lips, and the scent of her arousal surrounded him. He inhaled deeply, thanking whatever god had finally brought Alona to him.

"What are you doing?" she asked, her tone a little unsure.

"This." Leaning forward, he flattened his tongue and licked up the length of her pussy. "Delicious."

Before she could respond, he began licking her in earnest. She gripped his head, both for balance and to direct him to where she wanted him most. He homed in on her clit, wrapping his lips around the swollen bundle of nerves and sucking hard. Meanwhile, he slid one finger into her heat, pumping in and out of her.

Alona's legs quivered as a small orgasm moved through her body. He continued licking and sucking her until she pulled his hair to stop him.

"Jayden, quit fucking around, I need you inside me. Now."

He sat back on his heels with a smirk. "Whatever you want baby."

Apparently his girl wasn't a fan of foreplay. He'd have to change that. "Get on the bed," she ordered.

His cock twitched. God, he really loved her bossy side. He moved to lay on top of the soft comforter, putting his hands behind his head, his casual pose belying the excitement coursing through his body. Jayden watched as she crawled up the bed, heavy breasts swaying, until she was in a position to straddle him.

Alona reached over to the bedside table, reaching inside and pulling out a strip of condoms. He realized with a jolt that he'd not thought of protection at all, which was totally unlike him. He'd learned at an early age to keep things carefully wrapped. There were too many groupies who were hoping for a billionaire baby daddy to support them.

Ripping the condom package with her teeth, Alona freed the condom from its wrapper and quickly slid it down his length. Her confidence was hot as hell. Without another word, she adjusted her position, lined up his cock with her opening, and sank down on him with a long sigh of pleasure.

"Oh fuck, you're so warm and tight," he gritted out, his eyes rolling back in his head out of pure pleasure.

Bracing herself with her hands on his chest, Alona began moving up and down on his cock. She started slowly, then picked up speed. With every stroke, her large breasts bounced, mesmerizing him. Jayden bent his knees, bracing his feet on the bed to give him the leverage to meet her pace, and reached up to cup her breasts, one in each hand. He squeezed them softly and felt her internal muscles grip around his cock in response. It was heavenly.

Jayden had slept with a lot of women in his rock star days. For years Jayden and his brothers were surrounded by women enamored with their money, fame, and good looks. They never needed to ask, or even make an effort; the women offered themselves eagerly. He'd certainly taken advantage of those offers, more times than he could count.

But it never felt like this. He'd never felt like he was losing himself in another person. Not once in all the times he'd been with a woman had he felt this connection, this sensation that they were two halves of a whole finally coming together. Not until he found Alona. His woman. If she thought they were going to walk away after what he already knew was going to be the best sex of his life, she was crazy.

Alona was close, he could tell by the spasming of her internal muscles and the unfocused look in her eyes. He gripped her hips tightly and took control, bouncing her up and down his cock roughly, their bodies slamming together on every downward stroke.

"Ahhh! Jesus Christ! Jayden!"

Her eyes closed, her mouth opened wide in a silent scream, and she stiffened for just a moment before coming around him with more force than he'd known was possible. The orgasm visibly rolled through her whole body, coalescing where she gripped his dick with her internal muscles, keeping him deep inside her.

The look of pure pleasure on her face was enough to trigger his own orgasm, and he came with a shout, pushing up deep inside her and filling up the condom. For the first time in his life, he felt sad to be wearing a condom. He had a vision of Alona rounded with his child. He resisted asking her if she wanted a baby and instead hugged her tight as she collapsed on top of his chest, panting heavily.

Alona lifted her head, resting her chin on his chest so she could look up at him. She stared at him speculatively for a long moment.

"I want to renegotiate."

Alona

Alona looked across the table, studying Jayden as he slathered butter on a piece of toast. For someone who'd kept her up most of the night and given her half a dozen orgasms, he looked pretty energized. His hair was damp from the shower they'd taken together a while earlier, and now here he was, sitting in her kitchen wearing only his briefs. She suspected that there were millions of women who'd give anything to be in her place right now. She had to admit, it was an incredible sight.

They'd talked a lot since he came over yesterday, sharing their stories in more detail than they had before. It was easy to forget that Jayden was a billionaire former superstar. Surprisingly, he seemed really down to earth and practical. There was nothing prima donna or ostentatious about him. She'd expected that he'd be the type of person who would brag about all the famous people he knew, or name drop all the expensive things he owned. Instead, he talked about his family, in a way that told her clearly how much they meant to him and told her about some of the good work they'd done at the law firm. She could tell he was proud of that.

"Would you be interested in going to the street fair today?" Jayden asked.

"Street fair?"

"They're having one in the Loop this afternoon," he said, referring to a section of downtown. "I can't remember the theme, but I saw a flier at work and thought it sounded like fun. I haven't been to a street fair in years."

"Sure, that would be fun."

That was one of the great things about Chicago; during the summer there was a street fair or a festival every weekend somewhere in the city.

She tried not to think about how quickly she'd gone from wanting to have this day all to herself to wanting to spend it with Jayden, but she resolved just to go with it. The truth was that she'd been practical and responsible her entire life. For once, she just wanted to have fun. And Jayden Oliver clearly knew how to have fun.

"If it's okay I would like to stop at my place on the way there and get some clean clothes."

"Your house is on the way?" she asked curiously. "I assumed you lived in Lake Forest or something."

He shook his head.

"Too elitist for me. I have a townhouse by DePaul."

She tried not to show her shock that he lived in a neighborhood with regular people. "Sounds good."

Alona got dressed, pulling on a comfortable pair of jeans and a t-shirt emblazoned with the Ukrainian flag. Jayden's house was a quick El ride from her place and once again he surprised her. She figured someone like him would have a private car or at least want to Uber everywhere, not take the train like most Chicagoans did. It wasn't for show either, he had a monthly transit pass, the same as she did.

They exited at the DePaul station and walked a few blocks to his house. He lived on a shady street with rows of brick townhomes that shared a common backyard. She followed him inside, looking around curiously.

You would never know someone super wealthy lived here. She'd expected gold foil ceilings, marble floors, a dozen bedrooms, designer furnishings and maybe a butler or something. Instead, what she found was a clean and modest three-bedroom space, filled with family pictures, comfortable furniture, and lots of books neatly arranged on shelves. The only thing that looked like it cost a lot of money was a super fancy entertainment system with a giant TV, a stereo, and several gaming consoles, but that was the case at most bachelor apartments she'd visited.

She was examining the pictures on the mantle when Jayden returned, dressed in faded jeans, Nikes, and a light blue button down that brought out the color of his eyes. He stuck a baseball cap on his head, which just added to his boyish charm. He gestured to the picture in her hand, showing a happy-looking couple surrounded by four young boys and a serious looking older girl.

"That was the last picture of all of us with our parents before they died."

He pointed to another photo.

"Those are my grandparents, and that picture on the corner is all the Oliver siblings with their spouses and kids last summer. Those buildings in the background are part of our family farm."

She nodded as she returned the photo to the mantle. "Those kids are adorable."

"Yeah, I can't wait to go home and see them again."

"I really like your place," she told him honestly.

He smiled. "You sound surprised."

"I guess I'd just expected something big and ostentatious."

"That's not me, Alona."

She nodded. "I'm starting to see that."

"I'd rather use my money to do something good for the world, not buy a lot of useless crap that I don't need."

It was startling how closely their values were aligned. He stepped forward, pulling her into his arms and kissing her deeply. Her pulse skyrocketed, even as she reminded herself that she was already sore from their strenuous lovemaking the night before. And this morning. When he finally pulled away, his eyes were hooded with passion.

"We'd better go, love, before we never leave."

She laughed as she followed him out. She couldn't remember when she'd felt so comfortable with a guy, especially not so early in the relationship. She'd had three long-term boyfriends, and it had taken her months to feel this at ease with them.

There was something about Jayden, the way he made her feel like she was the focus of all his attention, the way he looked at her like she was the most beautiful woman he'd ever seen, that filled her with hope. As he threaded their fingers together and walked to the El station to head downtown, she only hoped this wasn't just a fantasy.

The next six weeks she and Jayden were practically inseparable. They talked and texted every day, spent every weekend together, and slept over at each other's houses several nights a week. The sex was off the charts, but they also liked to go for walks along the lakefront, go to outdoor events, and hang out reading or watching movies. They'd even gone to the theater to see Hamilton one night, which they'd both loved.

It was almost frighteningly easy for them to fold themselves into each other's lives. After a couple weeks of incessant hints from her mother, she had brought Jayden to dinner at her parents' house.

Mama had made him a traditional Ukrainian dinner, which he seemed to like, judging by the enormous amount of food he'd eaten. He'd been polite and charming, taking her mother's nosiness and unsubtle hints about knocking her up in stride. Jayden talked sports with Tato, and shared music gossip with her sister, who was way more interested in popular music than Alona was.

In between it all, they worked on planning the benefit concert. While they had a planning committee working with them, the bulk of the work was done by Jayden and Alona. They worked together well, bouncing ideas off of each other, and splitting duties. It was as if they'd planned a thousand events together.

It was going to be an incredible event. Jayden had pulled in his musical contacts and lined up an impressive array of musical talent, including one of her favorite bands from the eighties. To her surprise, every group had agreed to play for free as a way to support the cause. His brother-in-law Nick had volunteered his firm to manage event security, so that left Alona in charge of ticket sales and publicity.

With four weeks left before Ukrainian Independence Day, all of their tickets were sold out despite their high price. There was so much interest in the concert that Alona had worked out a deal to do a live simulcast in one of the parks on the lakefront, with reduced price tickets for the people watching the concert on screens outside. One of her board members had pulled some strings to allow local Ukrainian restaurants to sell food at the outdoor event instead of the vendors that the park district usually worked with. It was shaping up to be the event of the summer.

It seemed like everyone in the Chicago area was rallying behind the event, wanting to help the country her parents had been born in. It was a great feeling.

Also a great feeling? Falling asleep with Jayden's lean body wrapped around her. Alona had always been a practical woman, never one to daydream about weddings and babies like her friends. But in Jayden's arms, for the first time in her life, she allowed herself to dream about a happily ever after.

Jayden

The concert was coming up in two weeks. The musical acts were booked, the tickets were sold out, and the vendors were confirmed. There was only one thing left to do: practice.

It had been five years since he and his brothers had performed in front of a large crowd, and they were a bit rusty. The guys came into Chicago for the weekend and holed up in a local practice space, relearning their set list. The music itself was mostly muscle memory, but being apart for so long had impacted their timing and connection as performers. After two straight days of work though, they were back in the groove.

It was fun being back together with his brothers, who were all staying at his house for the weekend, but he also missed Alona. They'd texted throughout the weekend, but he missed seeing her in person. Missed waking up next to her. He even missed sitting on the couch with her and reading. God, he was so far gone for her.

He'd been clear about his feelings, even telling her that he loved her a few times, but even after six weeks together he had absolutely no idea how she felt about him. She was affectionate, but she held her feelings close to the vest. He was all in on this relationship, but he didn't know if she was there yet. She resisted talking about anything past the concert and ignored his subtle hints about taking a trip together or what they'd do for the holidays. He was starting to get nervous.

"Hey, how did you know that Janie loved you?" he asked Johnny, his oldest brother.

"When she got all jealous that time we ran into Simone at a party," he responded, referring to their former publicist who Johnny had dated for a while. "I suspected it before then, and of course I was already a goner for her. But when I saw how furious she was when Simone grabbed me and kissed me, well then I knew I was right, and she felt the same as me. Why do you ask?"

"You know I've been dating this woman Alona right?"

Johnny nodded. "Yeah, Jenny told me. Honestly, I'm surprised it took you this long to bring her up."

"Who?"

Their brother Justin handed them each a bottle of water and plopped down next to them.

"Jayden's lady love," Johnny told him.

"Hey Jim, we're finally getting the scoop on Jayden's girl," Justin called to their other brother.

"I can't believe you told Jen before us," he admonished as Jim hurried over to join them.

"Like any of us can keep a secret from Jen," Jayden responded wryly.

"Okay we're all here now. It's about time you talked to us," Johnny told him. "Now spill."

"My co-chair for the concert is this woman Alona, she works at the RUC," he began. "The minute I saw her, I felt kind of funny, but the first time our eyes met I knew, like at a cellular level or something, I just knew that she was the one for me. Boom. Love at first sight. For me anyway."

His brothers nodded.

"It was the same for me and Paige," Jim said.

"Me and Janie too," Johnny added.

"Paige and Janie hated you when they first met you," Jayden reminded them.

"They only thought they hated us," Johnny said smugly.

He knew that both of his brothers had a rocky start to their relationships. Justin, on the other hand, had a good start but a rocky middle that separated him and Peggy for many years before they found each other again. But each of his brothers, and his sister Jen, seemed really happy now that they were all married.

"Alona is kind of guarded. Cautious."

"Maybe she just needs some time," Johnny suggested.

"Or maybe she needs a grand gesture," Justin suggested. Justin was always the most romantic and sensitive of the brothers.

"Like what?" he asked.

"Ooh, I know," Johnny snapped his fingers excitedly. "You should write a song for her. Chicks love stuff like that."

"She's not really into our music," Jayden admitted.

They all looked at him like he'd said something crazy. After all, they'd been one of the most famous boy bands of their generation; pretty much everyone loved their music.

"What does she like then?"

"She likes 80s alternative music."

Justin shot him a look. "How old is this woman exactly?"

He laughed. "Three years older than me. Besides, I don't want to scare her off. She's kind of skittish. I think Johnny is right, she just needs some more time. Now let's get back to work, I'm starting to get hungry."

A couple of hours later the brothers headed to a local bar to get dinner and a couple of beers. They had all quit drinking so much their last year on tour, but they still enjoyed the occasional drink. Like so many unhealthy habits of their touring years, they'd learned the value of moderation. The guys found a table in the corner, then ordered burgers and a pitcher of beer to share.

They'd only been there a little while when a group of women stopped by their table, stars in their eyes. They looked like they were in their late twenties or early thirties, and clearly dressed up for a night out on the town with short skirts, lowcut tops, sky high heels, and enough makeup to obscure any natural beauty they had.

"Oh my God, you're the Oliver Boys!" one of them squealed. "Can we get some pictures? Or maybe we can join you?"

The brothers exchanged a look. They used to love this when they were younger, now not so much. But they all knew that the fans were responsible for their success, and a little give and take with them was necessary. Fortunately, this kind of thing happened less and less, especially since they all lived in different states now. They hadn't performed in five years and were rarely all together. The only reason that anyone noticed them anymore was because they were all together in public, that's when people connected the dots.

"Okay, we'll pose for some pictures," Johnny agreed, his voice kind but firm. As the oldest of the brothers, he'd always been the leader. "But then you'll need to move along."

"Are you sure you guys don't want to party? We're heading to this underground club that's supposed to be totally happening."

"Just a quick picture," Johnny reiterated. "We're discussing business tonight."

"Okay," the girl pouted. "Whatever."

The women crowded around them, calling out to a waitress to snap some photos on one of their phones. They squeezed in behind the brothers, leaning over them and resting their ample cleavage on their shoulders.

The woman behind Jayden giggled in his ear, whispering, "You're the single one, right?"

"I have a girlfriend," he answered.

"So?"

Jayden felt vaguely ill, wondering why they ever thought it was cool for women to hit on them like this. The woman snuggled closer, draping herself over Jayden and kissing him on the cheek just as the camera flashed. He leaned away.

"Hands off, sweetheart. Lips too."

She pouted, but moved away, leaving with her equally disappointed girlfriends. He breathed a sigh of relief.

The guys were on the El heading home to Jayden's place when the google alerts hit their phones.

"Oliver Boys Party Like the Old Days, Leaving Their Wives at Home for a Night of Partying in the Windy City as the Band Plans Their New Worldwide Tour."

Alona

The vibrating of her phone woke Alona up early the next morning. Squinting, she saw that she had a string of text messages and missed calls that had come in while she was sleeping, but she'd had her phone on silent. She frowned, wondering what was happening.

Jayden: *Please don't freak out. I swear it's not what it looks like. We only took a picture with them, then we told them to get away from us.*

Jayden: *I didn't know she was going to do that. I told her to stop touching me. There was absolutely no partying going on. The guys and I just stopped for dinner, nothing else, and they ambushed us. We went right home after. Please call me.*

Jayden: *You're probably sleeping, but please call me when you wake up.*

Jayden: *Are you awake yet? Call me.*

Olga: *Did you see the news? Is it true? I swear if it is I'll castrate him for you.*

Olga: *Warning, Mama and Tato saw the story. Tato is furious. He might fight me about who gets to do the castration.*

Jayden: *Are you mad? Can I please explain what happened? Hello?!?*

Mama: *Are you okay Alona? Should we come over?*

She sat up, completely confused. Pressing the speed dial, she called her sister.

"Hey Olga, I saw your texts, but I don't know what you're talking about."

Her sister's voice was cautious. "So, you didn't see the story?"

"What story?"

"There's a story on the Spill the Tea website about Jayden and his brothers partying with some skanky looking young girls last night."

"They don't do that anymore. Jayden said they gave up all the partying."

"There are pictures. I'm sorry Alona, but I thought you'd like to hear it from me first."

"Fuck. Okay, let me check it out. I'll call you later."

"Okay sis. I'm sorry. Let me know if you want me to come over with ice cream and whiskey later."

"I will, thanks."

Shooting off a quick text to her mother saying she was okay and would call her tonight after work, Alona pulled up the Spill the Tea website. Jayden and his brothers had made the top story of the gossip site. The headline screamed the news.

"Oliver Boys Party Like the Old Days, Leaving Their Wives at Home for a Night of Partying in the Windy City as the Band Plans Their New Worldwide Tour."

Underneath the headline was a series of pictures showing Jayden and his brothers at a bar, a pitcher of beer on the table, surrounded by five young women who'd draped themselves over the guys. They were all young, skinny, and dressed provocatively. One woman was resting her enormous breasts on Jayden's right shoulder, while planting a kiss on his cheek.

A flash of jealousy took her by surprise. She was not a jealous person. She looked at Jayden's texts again and then returned to the photo, blowing it up so she could get a better look at Jayden's face. He looked uncomfortable. As a matter of fact, all of the brothers looked uncomfortable and slightly repulsed. She breathed a sigh of relief. There must be more to the story.

She started to text Jayden, then stopped as she wondered how often this kind of thing happened. It made her slightly nauseous to think that she was with a guy who always had women flirting with him. Even if he hadn't wanted these girls, surely there would always be others. Why would he be with an older, chubby, boring Ukrainian girl if he could be with someone young, thin, and beautiful? Alona wasn't normally insecure, but something about seeing that picture made her feel like she was totally out of her league, and she didn't like that. Maybe her first instincts had been correct; the two of them were too different.

She skimmed the rest of the article. It said that the band had gotten back together and was working on a new album. It said they were performing at the Ukraine benefit concert as a way to kick off their next tour.

Wait a minute. The band was thinking about going back out on tour? Jayden hadn't said a word about that, but according to the article they were working with their manager to set up tour dates. She'd had no idea. He hadn't said a word. Alona felt a stab of pain behind her sternum, so sharp it was hard to breathe.

She'd managed to forget that she was dating a former superstar, but now it all came back to her. Sure, he was a lawyer now, but looking at the pictures, thinking about how excited he was about getting the band back together for the concert, it all made her wonder if the article was right. Despite him telling her how happy he was with his job and his life here in Chicago, clearly he still missed his old glamorous life, traveling around the globe. She wasn't surprised. How could a guy who'd played at the White House for the President be happy with a dull law career or hanging out with her watching movies?

She wondered when Jayden had been planning to tell her about the tour. She knew enough about major concert tours to know that he would be gone for months at a time. Was he thinking they were just a summer fling? It felt like so much more to her, and she'd thought they were on the same page there. He'd told her that he loved her several times, although she'd never said it back. Maybe he thought she'd wait for him and do a long-distance relationship while he gallivanted around the world. There was no way that would work for her.

Her phone buzzed with another text from Jayden.

Jayden: *Can I come over so we can talk? I'm so sorry about the article, but nothing happened.*

Alona: *I got your messages. My phone was off, and I didn't see them until I woke up just now. I saw the story and I'm not mad at you. I can tell* *that you are obviously uncomfortable with that girl hanging all over you in that picture.*

Jayden: *Totally. We all were super uncomfortable.*

Alona: *Does this kind of thing happen often? Women throwing themselves at you?*

Jayden: *Not as much as it used to, but yeah, we sometimes have fans who get a little overzealous. Get a little too close. It's the price of fame.*

Alona: *But I thought you left that life? Maybe you miss it, just a little?*

She watched anxiously as the little bubbles appeared and disappeared while he typed his response. Was he going to tell her about the tour now?

Jayden: *We didn't think anyone would even recognize us anymore. It's been five years since our last tour. We thought we could just have dinner without people bothering us.*

She noticed he hadn't answered her question about missing his old life. She waited to see if he'd add anything. Tell her about the tour. Let her know he was going on the road. His next text was like a knife to the heart.

Jayden: *I'm glad you understand how it is.*

Alona: *OK then, I need to get ready for work.*

Jayden: *Can I see you tonight?*

Alona: *No. I don't think that's a good idea.*

Jayden: *You said you weren't mad at me.*

Alona: *I'm not, but I have to be honest. This is a lot for me. I'm not used to guys I date being in the national gossip rags. It's kind of upsetting. I think I need to be alone for a while.*

Jayden: *It was upsetting for us too. My brothers all had to calm down their wives. How much time do you need?*

Alona: *I don't know. A while. This all reminded me that we're very different people with different values.*

Jayden: *We're not that different. You KNOW me, better than almost anyone.*

When she didn't respond, he sent another text.

Jayden: *What's happening? Are you breaking up with me?*

Alona: *I don't know. I need some time to think.*

Jayden: *Please, can we just talk?*

Alona: *Let's just focus on the concert for now. That's the most important thing.*

Jayden: *I love you.*

Alona: *I'll be in touch.*

Jayden

Jayden stared at his phone, willing it to ring. It had been five days since he'd heard from Alona. He'd told her that he loved her, and her only response had been that she'd be in touch. It was like a knife to the heart.

She'd emailed him updates about the concert but otherwise there had been no contact. He couldn't even insist on seeing her since the bulk of the work for the concert was already done.

He had no idea what she was thinking or how she was feeling. He missed her terribly. It was like a physical ache. Trying to respect her request to give her space was killing him. He knew he should just take a hint and let her go, but he couldn't do it. He loved her too much to let her go.

His phone buzzed and he nearly jumped out of his skin. He stifled a sigh of disappointment when he saw that it was his sister.

"Hey Jenny."

"Why do you sound like you lost your best friend?" she asked suspiciously, immediately picking up on his mood. His sister had helped raise him, and she was more like a mother than a sister to him and knew him better than even his brothers did.

"I think Alona broke up with me."

"You think?"

"She was upset about the picture and the article. I explained what happened, but she said she needed space and that she would contact me when she was ready. That was five days ago. I've heard nothing since then."

Jenny sighed. "I'm sorry Jay-Jay. That article was shit. Stupid gossip sites."

"She said she believed me when I told her I had nothing to do with that girl climbing all over me," he said. "Then she said she needed time because she wasn't used to dating someone who was in the gossip columns or had women hanging all over them trying to get close."

His sister chuckled. "Well, very few people are used to that. But it feels like there's more to the story somehow."

"I agree."

"You've got to go talk to her, little brother. I'm all for giving people space to process things, but too much time is bad too. Five days is too long to keep her stewing on whatever she's upset about."

"You're right Jenny."

"Yeah, I get that a lot."

Jayden smiled for the first time since he saw that damn Spill the Tea article. "I'm going to find her and make her talk to me."

"Good luck Jay-Jay. Let me know how it goes."

"I will. Bye."

As soon as Jayden was done with work, he headed over to Alona's apartment. Fortunately, it was Friday, and everyone pretty much left the office on time to start their weekend. Climbing the stairs to Alona's third-floor walk-up, he sent up a silent prayer to any god who was listening that he could fix this. He couldn't lose the woman he loved.

He knocked twice before she came to the door. She looked terrible. Her eyes were red-rimmed, her hair was a mess, and she was wearing a faded old t-shirt with food stains on it and holey sweatpants. He'd never loved her more.

"Jayden. What are you doing here?" Her voice was small and defeated.

"I know you said you needed time and well, I've given you some time. I miss you Alona. Can we please talk?"

Her response was a deep sigh, but she left the door open for him to follow her as she walked away. She dropped down on one side of the couch, gesturing for him to join her. Jayden sat on the coffee table facing her, his knees only an inch from hers.

"Nothing happened with that girl," he told her. "They were fans. We just posed for pictures, then told them to go away."

She nodded. "I know."

"I don't understand why you're so upset then."

Alona surged out of her seat so fast she almost knocked him over. She looked furious as she started pacing angrily across the room.

"You don't understand why I'm upset?" she said incredulously. "I mean, why would I be upset?"

She unleashed a string of what he suspected were Ukrainian swear words before switching back to English. Her voice increased in pitch the angrier she got.

"You're the one who pursued me, Jayden. I thought you and I had similar values. That we wanted the same things."

She waved her hands wildly as she stalked back and forth.

"You made me fall in love with you and now you're going on tour with your brothers and going back to your glamourous rock star lifestyle? And I'm supposed to do what? Hang out here and wait for you, ignoring all the pictures of you and whatever kind of slutty girls hit on rock stars? You really have some nerve."

Jayden's heart stopped, then restarted with a painful thump.

"You love me?" he whispered wonderingly.

She shot him a frustrated glare. "It doesn't matter. I'm not going to be some kind of rock concert widow. When exactly were you planning to tell me about this tour?"

He stood up and gently grabbed her by the shoulders, halting her pacing. "What are you talking about? I'm not going on tour. I have a job. A job I love."

She looked at him suspiciously. "The article said you were working on a new album and going on tour."

He started laughing and Alona gave him a look that clearly said she was about to stab him with the nearest sharp object.

"You can never believe anything you read in Spill the Tea, Alona. It's all bullshit. We're not going on tour. Even if any of us wanted to, which we don't, my brothers' wives would kill them for even considering it. Not to mention the fact that being apart from you for the last week damn near killed me. There's no way I could go on the road and leave you for months at a time."

She looked up at him, her expression vulnerable.

"You're not going back to being a rock star?"

"No honey, I'm not. I like being a lawyer, and I'm good at it. I like living anonymously and taking the El and going to street fairs and checking out hole-in-the-wall restaurants with you. My life is perfect just the way it is, especially now that I found you."

"Really?"

He nodded, bending his knees so he could meet her eyes.

"I love you Alona. You're it for me. I want to spend the rest of my life with you. Only you. Right here, in Chicago, doing boring coupley things."

Her face relaxed. "Oh my God, I was really freaked out."

"I know. So can we make up now, love?"

He leaned forward to kiss her, but she pushed him away. "I need to brush my teeth. I just stress ate a huge order of onion rings."

He gave her a tender smile. "I love you even when you have onion breath."

She reached up to wrap her hands around his neck. "I love you too Jayden."

"Let's never be apart so long again," he requested. "I hate it."

She nodded. "You've got a deal."

Epilogue – Alona

One year later...

"And now, performing a special set to support Ukrainian rebuilding efforts, everyone's favorite band, The Oliver Boys!"

The crowd went crazy, cheering as Jayden and his brothers took the stage. Alona couldn't help but feel proud as she saw her handsome boyfriend grab his guitar and wave to the crowd. He was dressed in skinny jeans and a shirt that he'd left unbuttoned, displaying his toned chest. She knew every woman in the place was ogling Jayden and his brothers, but she didn't care. They could look all they wanted to, he was still hers.

Other than at last year's Ukraine benefit, she'd only seen the band perform one other time. Last Christmas they'd all gone to Kansas and the guys had put on an impromptu concert for their family and friends at the tiny bar where they'd first been discovered all those years ago. True to his word, neither Jayden nor his brothers had any interest in going back out on tour. They loved doing these reunion shows for charity though.

"Let's move closer to the stage."

Jayden's sister Jen grabbed her arm, dragging her around to the side of the stage. She'd gotten to know Jen pretty well over the past year that she'd been dating Jayden and she really liked her, even if she was pushier and nosier than her own mother – which was saying a lot. Mama and Jen had gotten along like best friends when her family came to Kansas with Alona and Jayden for Christmas last year. No one had been safe from their interrogations.

The crowd cheered as the band finished their first song and started the next. They played a couple more songs before Jayden moved to the mic.

"The boys and I have been working on a new song," he started, stopping as the crowd went crazy, hooting and hollering.

Alona raised her eyebrow. Jayden had never mentioned that they had a new song. She thought they told each other everything.

"I wrote this song for someone special," Jayden continued.

His eyes found hers in the crowd.

"Someone I love. Someone who makes me a better man. Someone I hope to spend the rest of my life with."

The crowd freaked out again, while Jayden and Alona stared at each other like they were the only people there. The music started and Jayden began singing to her.

My Ukrainian princess. The woman of my dreams.
Your love made me whole. Set me free.
My Ukrainian princess. The one I adore.
You complete me. Marry me.

Alona's eyes filled with tears as he repeated the verse in perfect Ukrainian, before gesturing for her to join him on stage.

"Your mom helped him with that," Jen told her as she dragged her towards the stairs leading up to the stage. Jen's husband Nick gave her a wink as he moved aside to let her ascend the stairs. Jayden walked over to her, still singing. He finished the verse and dropped to one knee, holding out an engagement ring. She fell to her knees next to him, tears streaming down her face.

"Alona, my Ukrainian princess," Jayden's voice boomed over the speakers. "Will you do me the honor of marrying me?"

She nodded.

"Is that a yes?" he asked.

"Yes!"

The crowd went crazy again as Jayden pulled her in for a long kiss. When they broke apart, he slipped the ring on her finger, and she admired the beautiful ring. It was antique looking with a small diamond surrounded by blue and yellow stones that were reminiscent of the Ukrainian flag. She loved it.

Jayden pulled her to her feet and whispered in her ear, "Wait for me backstage? I want to have my way with you after we finish this set."

She nodded. "I'll wait for you forever Jayden Oliver."

***

Thank you for reading Jayden and Alona's story. If you want to read about how the rest of the Oliver siblings find love, check out the Oliver Boys Rockstar Romance series, available now at all major online bookstores. Jayden's boss Dave is also featured in the book Together Again. For these and other stories, visit my website at bit.ly/AuthorRoseBak[1].

If you liked this book, please show me some love, and leave a review. Good reviews are like puppies, they make everyone feel happy.

Keep reading for a special excerpt from "Until You Came Along", available everywhere now.

---

1. https://bit.ly/AuthorRoseBak

Special Preview

Until You Came Along by Rose Bak

Jen heard the rumbling from all the way in the kitchen. Wiping her hands on a towel, she walked to the front porch to watch the two large buses drive up the long driveway to the farmhouse. Belching smoke, they idled and came to a stop, one behind the other.

Although it wasn't even 10 a.m. yet, the sun shone brightly in the summer sky, showcasing the dust left in the wake of the parked buses. A bird squawked loudly in the sudden silence as a serious looking young woman scurried out of the first bus, glasses askew, a clipboard gripped in one hand, cellphone in another. Two large mountains of men followed her, hulking shadows.

"Jen Oliver? The band is here. We'll just come in and...." she moved to enter the house, but Jen stood her ground, blocking the door.

"Where are they?" she asked the woman, her tone icy. "And who are you exactly?"

The woman looked flustered for a brief moment before her stern mask fell back down again. She shuffled her cell phone into the hand with the clipboard and stuck out her now-free hand to shake. "I'm Simone. I manage the band."

Jen ignored her hand. "Well, manage them out of those buses. They don't get to send the help out to greet their sister."

Simone looked confused as she dropped her hand back to her side. "They're all sleeping. They had a late night. We'll just come in and check...."

"Still up all night and sleeping all day, huh? That's been the same since they were teenagers." Jen shook her head. On the farm they had all been taught the value of hard work – up before dawn, work all day, and early to bed. Somehow those lessons hadn't really stuck with her brothers despite her grandparents' best efforts over the years.

Of course, the boys, as she still thought of them, had been away from the farm for ten years now, chasing fame and fortune as the biggest boy band to hit the charts since N Sync. Like the band that came before them, the Oliver Boys had grown up but continued to enchant teenage girls across the world with their pop tunes.

Simone clearly felt protective of the boys. "They played last night in Wichita you know," she said sternly. "The show went until almost midnight, then they met the fans and press for hours after."

"By meet the fans and press do you mean got drunk and partied?" Jen's tone did little to hide her opinion of the boys and their reputation for debauched partying.

Simone shook her head. "They've mostly settled down now. There's not as much partying as there used to be when they were younger. But they still need to make an effort to meet people, it's part of the job. Now we'll just come in and...."

Jen shook her head. "Well," she drawled. "When they wake up from their so-called job, you send them on in. The rest of you need to find some other place to bunk. I'm not running a hotel for drunken roadies here."

A slight movement behind Simone caught Jen's eyes. One of the giant men flanking Simone shook with repressed laughter, his mouth twisted in a smirk but his face otherwise impassive. Jen looked at him for the first time. He was the size of a small tank, several inches over six feet tall, with impossibly wide shoulders and large biceps. His hair was a dark blond, "dishwater blonde" her grandma would call it, worn military short. He was dressed all in black, and she noticed a gun on the shoulder holster. Jen wondered why he felt he needed a gun out here in the middle of nowhere. She felt him watching her and she raised her eyes to his, a shiver of awareness coursing through her, although she couldn't make out his eyes behind the dark sunglasses.

"Miss Oliver..." Simone started again.

"Jen"

"OK, then, Jen, we need to do a security sweep before the boys come in. If you could just move aside, we'll get started." Simone nodded decisively.

"A security—-what the hell are you talking about?"

Simone turned to the man who'd been staring at Jen earlier. "This is Nick, he's head of security for the band. He'll be doing a security sweep and assessment with Brian here," she pointed at the second silent man.

"We don't need a security sweep. This place is as safe as it comes. We don't even lock the doors in these parts."

Simone shook her head again, vibrating with irritation and clearly not used to people disobeying her orders. "No way. The boys don't go anywhere without a security check ahead of time. I'm afraid I have to insist."

Jen shot her a look filled with venom, her tone as cold as ice. "You can insist all you like but this is my property. You have no right to it, and neither do the boys. Y'all can just run along now, I'm not having some ginormous strangers poking around my property. Don't make me sic the dogs on you." Simone's mouth dropped open.

This was an empty threat. Jen's three dogs looked mean, but they were incurably friendly. They were just as likely to lick a person to death as bite them. Jen had a sneaking suspicion that if someone tried to kill her the dogs would jump over her body and leave with the killer. But these music people didn't need to know that. If there was one thing Jen hated, it was music people. They were way too self-important and proud.

"Excuse me ma'am," the guy called Nick interrupted.

"Jen," she repeated, a trace of irritation in her tone.

He inclined his head. "Sorry. Jen. As Simone mentioned, I'm head of security for the band. We've had some issues and I would be very appreciative if my team could just poke around for a bit and make sure there's nothing amiss." His tone was deferential and charming, which only heightened Jen's suspicions.

"What kind of issues?"

"I'm afraid I'm not at liberty to discuss that ma—I mean Jen."

"Then I'm afraid I'm not at liberty to grant you access to my property. You step foot off that driveway, and I'll shoot you myself, right after I set the dogs on you. And you," she pointed at Simone, "better make sure no one bothers me again until I see those boys on my porch." She spun on her heel and slammed the door. It was going to be a long day.

***

For more of Jen's story, check out Until You Came Along by Rose Bak. Available at select online retailers.

Other Books by Rose Bak

Boozy Book Club Series
Beach Reads
Bubbly & Billionaires
Martinis & Mysteries
Bourbon & Bikers
Midlife Madness
Extra Innings
The Good with Numbers Holiday Romance Series
Love Unmasked
The Thanksgiving Scrooge
Maid for Christmas
Countdown to Love
Valentine's Lottery
Christmas Angel
Bite-Sized Shifters Paranormal Romance Series
Long Distance Wolf
Wolf Doctor
Kat's Dog
Designer Wolf
Wolf Sheriff
Cocktail Wolf
Second Chance Wolf
The Oliver Boys Band Contemporary Romance Series
Until You Came Along
Rock Star Teacher
Rock Star Writer
Rock Star Neighbor
Rock Star Lawyer
Loving the Holidays Contemporary Romance Series
Dating Santa

New Year's Steve

Independence Dave

Comfort & Joy

Holidays with the Shifters Series

Santa's Claws

Bear Humbug

Jingle Bear

Silver Paws

Joy to the Wolf

Lion's Heart

The Diamond Bay Contemporary Romance Series

Brand New Penny

Fresh as a Daisy

Right as Rain

Reunited Series

Together Again

Finding My Baby

Standalones

Beach Wedding

Jessie's Girl

Summer Wedding

Faking It with the Detective

Roasting with Rob

Halloween Surprise

Christmas Punch

King of the Reunion

Disaster Planning

Non-fiction

What to Do If You Find a Cougar in Your Living Room: Self-Care in an Uncaring World

It's All About Relationships: Reflections on Love, Friendship, and Connection

Catch up with these and other stories coming soon. For more information, join my newsletter at https://bit.ly/rosebaknewsletter, or follow my author page on your favorite retailer.

About the Author

Rose Bak has been obsessed with books since she got her first library card at age five. She is a passionate reader with an e-reader bursting with thousands of beloved books.

Although Rose enjoys writing both fiction and nonfiction, romance novels have always been her favorite guilty pleasure, both as a reader and an author. Rose's contemporary romance books focus on strong female characters over thirty-five and the alpha males who love them. Expect a lot of steam, a little bit of snark, and a guaranteed happily ever after.

Rose lives in the Pacific Northwest with her family, and special needs dogs. In addition to writing, she also teaches accessible yoga and loves music. Sadly, she has absolutely no musical talent, so she mostly sings in the shower.

Please sign up for the Rose Bak Romance newsletter at bit.ly/rosebaknewsletter[1] to get a free book and keep up to date on all the latest news. You can also follow Rose on Facebook[2], Instagram[3], Twitter[4], Goodreads[5], or Bookbub[6].

---

1. https://bit.ly/rosebaknewsletter
2. https://www.facebook.com/AuthorRoseBak
3. https://www.instagram.com/authorrosebak/
4. https://twitter.com/AuthorRoseBak
5. https://www.goodreads.com/authorrosebak
6. https://www.bookbub.com/authors/rose-bak

Don't miss out!

Visit the website below and you can sign up to receive emails whenever Rose Bak publishes a new book. There's no charge and no obligation.

https://books2read.com/r/B-A-VATM-ETBDC

BOOKS2READ

Connecting independent readers to independent writers.